Oliver Wilson Davis

Sketch of Frederic Fernandez Cavada

A native of Cuba: showing partially what one of his friends knew of him as

a soldier, a gentleman, a poet, a diplomat, an author, a patriot and a

victim

Oliver Wilson Davis

Sketch of Frederic Fernandez Cavada
A native of Cuba: showing partially what one of his friends knew of him as a soldier, a gentleman, a poet, a diplomat, an author, a patriot and a victim

ISBN/EAN: 9783337309237

Printed in Europe, USA, Canada, Australia, Japan

Cover: Foto ©Raphael Reischuk / pixelio.de

More available books at **www.hansebooks.com**

FREDERIC FERNANDEZ CAVADA,

A NATIVE OF CUBA.

———•———

SHOWING PARTIALLY WHAT ONE OF HIS FRIENDS KNEW OF HIM AS A
SOLDIER, A GENTLEMAN, A POET, A DIPLOMAT, AN AUTHOR,
A PATRIOT AND A VICTIM.

———•———

PRINTED FOR PRIVATE CIRCULATION.

PHILADELPHIA:
JAMES B. CHANDLER, PRINTER, 306 & 308 CHESTNUT STREET, PHILADELPHIA.

1871.

INTRODUCTION.

For the following sketch I have no apology to make, though fully aware of its imperfections. Am conscious, too, that what has been written renders me amenable to the charge of egotism. As this could not be avoided "I accept the situation"—from necessity.

If any one supposes the following pages to be a sketch of the life of Frederic F. Cavada, he will find out his error before he reads very far. It is only a statement of what I knew about him, and I have prepared it solely for the information of those gentlemen who, under the belief he was alive, aided me in trying to save his life, that they may understand why I was so persistent in the demands made upon them the fourth and fifth of July.

The life of Cavada has yet to be written, and if his record ever falls into the hands of a biographer whose pen is equal to that of William Wirt, when he wrote the life of Patrick Henry, it will be charming as a romance of real life, and instructive as a lesson. The incidents of his life of which I have any knowledge, cover only the short period of ten years—from July, 1861, when he was commissioned as a Captain in the Union Army, to July, 1871, when he was executed at Puerto Principe. Whoever will take the trouble to read the following pages must admit that he was a remarkable man.

The sketch has at least one merit—*"truth."* Though it has been prepared *within three days,* I have authority for all that is said :—the originals of letters and telegrams, and the testimony of *living* men to corroborate, if necessary, what has been written. I have not written a word with the expectation of aiding the cause of Cuba or bringing Spain into contempt. I have no interest in Cuba beyond that which any man must feel for a weak people striving to rid themselves of what they consider a tyranny, nor have I any cause of quarrel with Spain. Her representatives in Cuba have, it is true, killed a brave man, in violation of what I believe to be the laws of civilization, but this was not done by Spain. When her War Minister was appealed to, he directed that the charges against Cavada should be forwarded to Madrid for investigation.

It is not my intention to censure or criticise even by implication, the policy our government has adopted towards the Cuban Revolutionists. I did not approach General Grant or Mr. Fish as office holders, but as individuals whose intercession I sought in behalf a brave man, to whom fate had been unpropitious. Their hearts prompted them to do what they did, and on reflection I hope their judgment will not censure their action.

This pamphlet therefore has no *literary* pretensions or *political* meaning,—it is purely personal. If anybody is hurt by what has been written, it is his own fault. He should not have crossed Cavada's path. If he has done so, he has learned the lesson that the jackass did when he kicked a sleeping lion believing he was dead. The fable says that the lion awoke, and when the jackass went home, he left his ears behind him. The application is appropriate even if the fable be false.

The criticism may be made—" why should so much pains be taken to print a pamphlet about Cavada, and to tell what efforts were made to save his life, when those efforts were fruitless?" They resulted in nothing it is true, but they were made under the belief that he was alive on the fourth and fifth of July. They were promoted by such men as Gen. Graham, Gen. Sheridan, Gen. Meade, Gen. Horace Porter, Gen. Van Vliet, Moses Taylor, Samuel Sloan, John Hoey, Edward S. Sanford, John W. Forney and Gen. Sickles. As these gentlemen had committed themselves to Cavada's interest by one good action promptly done, is it not probable that they would have followed it up until they saw Cavada restored to his friends and family?

This sketch has been prepared for their information, and has been printed (not published) that they may know something of the man for whose life they were induced to intercede.

O. WILSON DAVIS.

New York, July 25th, 1871.

EARLY LIFE.

FREDERIC FERNANDEZ CAVADA was born in 1832, at Cienfuegos, Cuba. His father was a native of Cuba and died when Fred. was a mere boy. His widowed mother soon afterwards returned with her young family to Philadelphia, her native city. Fred. was first placed at school in Wilmington, Delaware, and after remaining there a few years, completed at Philadelphia all the education he ever received.

His health was always delicate, and when an opportunity offered, his mother yielded to his wish to accompany the surveying expedition to the Isthmus under Col. Trautwine, to survey the route for the Panama Railroad. At that time the "Chagres fever" was unknown, and his friends hoped that a life out of doors would build up his constitution; they also thought it would be a good opportunity for him to become a civil engineer if he developed any taste or talent for the profession.

He remained with the expedition until the survey was completed, and returned home with Col. Trautwine. The malarious swamps of the Isthmus had not improved his health, but on the contrary had planted in his system the seeds of disease which followed him through life.

His first care was the restoration of his health, and for several years he spent a life of comparative ease, reading, writing, sketching, and thinking as inclination prompted him. When the rebellion broke out, in April, 1861, he was anxious to enlist for the "three months service," but his health was so delicate that his physician and friends dissuaded him from his intention. After the developments of April, May and June, 1861, had proved that there was to be a protracted struggle, Cavada resolved to take part in spite of his health.

ENLISTMENT.

During the "three months service," David B. Birney, of Philadelphia, was Lieutenant-Colonel of the Twenty-third Regiment of Pennsylvania Volunteers, of which Charles B. Dare was the Colonel. The writer was Birney's partner, and on July 15th, 1861, Birney wrote him from camp, near Williamsport, Maryland.

"I have determined to return to the service for three "years. General Cameron (then Secretary of War,) has "authorized me to raise a large regiment of fifteen com-"panies, to be divided into three battalions, as in the "French service. Colonel Dare is so far gone with the "consumption that he will be unable to return. I will "be the Colonel of the new regiment.

"As you are aware, the term of our enlistment will
"expire in a few days, and I had hoped to be able to
"return home then, but General Patterson wishes us to
"remain longer, and the men have consented to do so.
"We may be here a month, but I do not wish in the
"meantime to delay the organization of the new regi-
"ment. You had some experience in raising the pre-
"sent regiment, and why can you not take hold and
"start a new regiment to serve for three years, before
"the ardor of the boys has time to abate?

"Do this, and I will send you the requisite authority.
"If you go to work in earnest, you should have the
"regiment almost ready by the time we return. A
"majority of the men in the present regiment will, I
"think, re-enlist for three years. If they do, many of
"them will return with me. After these are added to
"the men you raise, the new regiment should be ready
"to take the field in a few days after my return. This
"will prevent us from loafing about Philadelphia."

On this suggestion I acted, and on the seventeenth day
of July, 1861, rented the Girard House for a recruiting
office. It was the second largest hotel in Philadelphia,
and happened at the time to be vacant. Owing to the
liberality of George G. Presbury, Esq., the lessee, the
rent was nominal.

The location and size of the recruiting office attracted
some attention, and in a few days there were numerous

applicants from among the young men of Philadelphia, for positions as line officers in the new regiment. As the writer was entirely ignorant of military matters, and as the applicants were equally ignorant. the position of both parties was somewhat embarrassing. The only criterion which, under the circumstances, it was possible to adopt, was previous knowledge of the applicant, and in the absence of this, then a decision could only be made from impressions produced by personal appearance and a few moments conversation.

On the twentieth day of July, 1861, a delicate looking young man entered the business office of the writer, and asked for a position in the Twenty-third Pennsylvania Volunteers.

" What position ?" was the question.

Answer—" First or Second Lieutenant."

" Do you live in Philadelphia ?"

" Yes."

" Born here ?"

" No."

" Where ?"

" In Cuba, but educated here."

" What knowledge have you of military matters ?"

" None whatever, but I think I could soon qualify myself for a subordinate position. I will, of course, defray my portion of the expense of raising my company, if I can get a position."

"Can you go to work *at once?*"

"Yes, and I have already about a dozen men who have promised to go in my company."

"What's your name ?"

"Frederic Cavada."

"What is your business ?"

"Nothing. I was engaged on the survey of the Panama Railroad, but since I returned home, have been unable to do any work on account of my health."

"Do you think you could endure the exposure of a soldier's life ?"

"I do not know, but have made up my mind to try it."

The quiet but resolute manner of my new acquaintance, his ready and pertinent answers, and his general appearance, so impressed me that I felt I had drawn a prize. After a few moments reflection, I said :

"You can go as captain if you wish to ?"

Cavada replied : "I should like to do so very much, but did not expect it. As you do not know me, perhaps you would like to have letters from my friends to tell you who I am."

"Never mind who you are. I think you will do. Do not trouble yourself about the letters, but go to work. Take a room in the Girard House and raise your company as soon as possible."

He did so, and in three days his company was full and ready to be mustered into the service.

SERVICE AS CAPTAIN.

The "three months" Twenty-third Pennsylvania Volunteers returned to Philadelphia on August 17th, 1861. Abut six hundred men of the new regiment met their future comrades at the Baltimore depot, and escorted them to the headquarters of the new regiment. The next day, Lieutenant Colonel Birney put all the men in camp at the corner of Nicetown Lane and Lamb Tavern Road, about four miles from the city, and began to organize the new regiment.

On Sunday, August 20th, the Secretary of War issued an order requiring all companies, that had been mustered in, to come to Washington. Birney went down early on Monday, August 21st, with all the men who were in camp, and completed the organization of the regiment at the Capitol.

When the regiment went to the Peninsula under McClellan, Cavada was detailed for duty as engineer. His talent for sketching and his knowledge of topography made him more useful, to the Generals under whom he served, as an engineer than as a line officer. Part of his duties on the Peninsula were performed in balloons, which, it will be remembered, were then used as the eyes of the Army of the Potomac. After the Peninsula campaign, he served with his regiment during the campaign under General Pope during August, 1862, and subsequently was in the battle of Antietam under General McClellan, September 17th, 1862.

SERVICES

AS

LIEUTENANT-COLONEL.

During the fall of 1862, the "One Hundred and Fourteenth Regiment of Pennsylvania Volunteers" was organized and Cavada was commissioned as Lieutenant-Colonel. He served as such at Fredericksburg in December, 1862, under Burnside, and at Chancellorsville in May, 1863, under Hooker.

At the battle of Gettysburg, July, 1863, Cavada had command of the regiment, the Colonel being absent.

The regiment was in the Brigade of General Charles K. Graham, and in the Division of General Birney, all which were in the Third Corps, commanded by General Sickles. General Meade was in command of the army. To all these Generals, Cavada was well known. How they appreciated him will appear subsequently.

A PRISONER.

At the battle of Gettysburg, Cavada and his Brigade Commander, General Charles K. Graham, were captured and taken to Libby Prison, at Richmond, Virginia. Cavada remained a prisoner of war until January, 1864, when he was released on parole. Even in Libby Prison he could not be idle. He cheated the long hours of their weariness by writing sketches of prison life, and illustrating them with designs from his pencil. As there was no stationer's store attached to the prison, he was compelled to write these sketches and draw the designs upon the margins of newspapers and such other scraps of paper as fell in his way.

When he was released, these multifold manuscripts, written on both sides of the sheet, escaped confiscation, because they were concealed between the shoes and stockings of the author and such of his comrades, who had taken an interest in his authorship, as were willing to incur the risk of further detention by concealing such documents upon their persons. According to the rules of the prison they were *contraband* of war.

These sketches and illustrations were, in 1864, published by King & Baird, of Philadelphia, in a book entitled "Libby Life." It is not, perhaps, quite equal as a literary production to "Picciola or the Prison Flower," by X. B. Saintine; but then it must be remembered that Saintine was a scholar while Cavada was only a soldier; besides this, "Chillon," where Saintine was imprisoned, was clean and comparatively so healthy a spot, that a "prison flower" could exist there, while the atmosphere of "Libby," where Cavada spent his term, was destructive not only of vegetable, but nearly all animal life. Only a small portion of the prisoners who were caged there ever survived, and they had for companions of their imprisonment numerous members of animated creation too repulsive to describe, and not possessing the attraction which the prisoner of "Chillon" found in the little flower.

A DUELLIST.

On his return to Philadelphia, emaciated by confinement, Cavada learned that in his absence, his Colonel had charged him with cowardice at the battle of Gettysburg, though, as already stated, the Colonel was not present during any portion of the engagement. Among other allegations, it was said that Cavada had permitted himself to be captured.

These reports naturally produced a revivifying effect upon the invalid soldier, who attempted to get an explanation from his Colonel. Failing in this, he foolishly challenged him. By some means these facts became known to General George Cadwalader, who was at the time in command at Philadelphia. As duelling was in violation not only of the Laws of Pennsylvania, but of the rules of the service, the General determined to put a stop to any further proceedings of the sort. The first step he took was to direct his Adjutant-General to forward a notice to Lieutenant-Colonel Cavada that he must consider himself under close arrest within the precincts of the Continental Hotel, so long as he remained in Philadelphia.

This order Cavada showed to the writer a few hours after its receipt, who took him to General Cadwalader's headquarters and introduced him. After an inspection of his personal appearance, the General relieved him from "close arrest," because he did not think Cavada a very dangerous man in the condition his health was at the time, and because he thought that it would be better for the service for Cavada to spend his leisure time in trying to repair his health, so that he might be able to go to duty in the field whenever he was exchanged.

A STAFF OFFICER.

During the month of March, Cavada was duly exchanged, but his delicate health and the depressing effect produced upon his spirits by the reports of his cowardice, had decided him to resign his commission. He made known his intention to his friends, who dissuaded him from his purpose, by offering to secure him a position on the Staff of General Birney, then in command of a division in General Hancock's Corps. This position was secured and Cavada served on General Birney's Staff during General Grant's campaign from Fredericksburg to Petersburg.

General Birney died in October, 1864. After his death Cavada resigned, having determined to go to Cuba, and perhaps South America, to try to recover his health.

UNITED STATES CONSUL.

———————

After his resignation had been accepted, Cavada made arrangements to leave the country. One afternoon as the writer was hurrying home from his office, to prepare to go to Washington at 4 o'clock, on business, he met Cavada, who said:—

"While I am away I do not wish to be idle, and I think I could serve the government during my absence in some way, perhaps in a semi-diplomatic capacity.

"Many complicated questions have arisen in South America. In some of these the government may be involved. I think I understand these questions, and may be of service to the State Department if I go to South America. If on my return to Cuba, I find the state of things existing which I am told exists there, I will remain in Cuba. In this event I know I can serve the government.

"I want no office, but would like before I start to have an interview with Mr. Seward."

The reply was:—

" Cavada, I know nothing about South American questions or Cuban affairs, but if you want to see the Secretary of State, I think I can procure an interview for you. I do not know Mr. Seward personally, but I know many gentlemen who are acquainted with him. I am going to Washington at 4 o'clock this afternoon, and the best thing you can do is to go with me."

Cavada answered—" I will meet you at the depot."

He did so, and we went to Washington. The next morning we went to the State Department, and fortunately met in the corridor, Edward S. Sanford, Esq., of New York. I introduced Cavada to him and telling him what we wanted, he immediately procured us an interview with Mr. Seward which lasted about an hour.

When we took leave, Mr. Seward said—" Colonel, I am very glad to have seen you. I will think of your suggestions and if I can make use of your services, you will hear from me."

In a few days, Cavada received from the State department the appointment of Consul for the United States at Trinidad de Cuba.

Shortly after his arrival he wrote the following letter, which it must be remembered was written only for a friendly eye, without any expectation that it would be seen in print:

CIENFUEGOS, CUBA,
January 17*th*, 1865.

O. WILSON DAVIS, ESQ.,
      Philadelphia.

DEAR SIR:

I send enclosed the lines, founded upon the incident at General Birney's grave, which you expressed a desire to see. I think their only merit consists in the endeavor to perpetuate an incident which proves how much honor is due to the memory of our lamented friend.

The sketch of the battle on the North Anna is very crude, but an intelligent artist might so arrange it as to present a fair picture of the action without departing much from local correctness in the details. I had intended drawing it out for you, together with some others, before leaving Philadelphia, but I was so much indisposed for several days previous to my departure, that I felt utterly unfit to undertake it.

I am happy to be able to say that since my arrival here, my health has improved wonderfully. I hope by the coming spring to return to the States with fully renewed strength and in better spirits.

The public mind here is deeply engrossed with the political events which are following each other so rapidly in the American Republic. Although not altogether unprepared for the lively interest taken in the war, I was nevertheless, not a little surprised to find this element of social excitement so extensively developed. Every one appears fully awake to the importance of the issues at stake. The abolition element is, strange to say, not limited to those who are not slave-holders, even some of the large slave owners being numbered among the proselytes of the new faith. The ultimate extinction of the institution of slavery over the whole Western Hemisphere, seems to be accepted as an inevitable sequel to its extinction in the United States. The colored population of this Island are not in the dark as to these great issues. Slavery, once abolished in the American Union as the resolution of the great problem which is now being evolved there, it will be scarcely possible that Cuban slavery, so near a neighbor to American liberty, could be maintained intact. The opinion seems daily to be losing ground, that the white race cannot labor in the fields of Cuba. The strongest argument upon which this theory was based, seems to have been the fact that the white race never *had* labored in the fields. The admission of the physical superiority of the negro in this respect is neither a safe one to the institution of slavery, nor to the permanent domination of the white race in intertropical climates. Would not a different system of physical education render the white laborer as impervious to the malignant effects of the sun as the African? This question begins to attract considerable attention here since the outbreak of the rebellion. "Let us be regenerated," say some, "or we are lost."

I doubt if the various movements of the armies, and their probable results, are discussed and speculated upon even in the States with more warmth and interest than they are here. There are many enthusiastic "Federals," who are constantly engaged in violent controversies with the rankest sort of "Confederates." After the late glorious victories of Thomas, and the splendid military promenade of Sherman, the "Secesh" kept themselves considerably in the back ground, and although the withdrawal of the Butler-Porter expedition from the waters of the Cape Fear, encouraged them to come feebly forth again to the charge, we trust that before long we may compel them to bury their arguments and expectations beyond the hope of resurrection.

It may appear surprising to you that there should exist here such warm sympathies with the Union cause. If Cuba belongs geographically to America, why should she belong politically to Europe? This question naturally suggests to the Cuban the fact that one day their Island must attach itself to the destinies of the American family. Commanding as it does the waters of the

Gulf of Mexico, which furnishes the seaboard of the Gulf States, possessing splendid harbors and rich lands, and counting its negro slaves by hundreds of thousands, it would no doubt be destined to fall a prey to Southern policy and Southern cupidity should the Confederacy establish its independence. But it is not overlooked here that the doctrine of State Rights in accordance with which such a Confederacy must be framed, would involve the constant peril of disunion and of anarchy, and in such an event what could be the ultimate fate of Cuba but that of St. Domingo and Jamaica? It would be too dangerous to try such a political experiment here, a country where the negro population outnumbers the white.

But this letter has already trespassed enough upon your time. I am apt to forget that Cuban politics and Cuban interests are not so interesting to others as they are to myself.

I remain,

Very truly your ob't servant,

F. F. CAVADA.

———

"The sketch of the battle on the North Anna" referred to in the foregoing letter, was a drawing prepared by Cavada at the request of the writer, who was then engaged upon the "Life of General Birney." The book was subsequently published, but without any sketches of battles in which Birney had been engaged, as had been originally designed, so that the drawing sent by Cavada was never used.

A POET.

The incident upon which Cavada based the verses referred to in the foregoing letter, occurred at the grave of General Birney, who was buried in "Woodlands Cemetery," Philadelphia, not far from the "Satterlee Hospital." The hospital was then filled with convalescent soldiers, principally from the army of the Potomac. After the troops which formed the funeral escort, the citizens, and the family had returned home, the writer remained at the grave to see that the workmen of the cemetery performed their duty properly. When the work was nearly completed, he saw through the dim twilight a soldier on crutches, who was intently watching the grave diggers. He said to him, "my man, what are you doing here?"

He replied, "I served, sir, under General Birney, and lost my leg in front of Petersburg. The stump has not yet healed, so that I could not attend the funeral, but I got leave of absence from the hospital to come over here."

After some further conversation the soldier hobbled away and the writer subsequently related the incident to Cavada. After he had gone to Cuba, I heard of the verses and had asked for a copy, which was enclosed with " the sketch of the battle on the North Anna."

They were the following:

BIRNEY'S GRAVE.

The solemn sounds were hushed ;
The martial music and the tolling bell,
The plaintive beating of the muffled drums,
And the echoed volleys of the funeral guns ;
And from the new made grave, where slept
The hero of many battles, all were gone—
All save one, for as the twilight came
Shrouding the silent grave-yard in the pall
Of falling night, there lingered still
An humble soldier leaning on his crutch.
Oh, who shall say what stirring thoughts they were
That stayed him at his chieftain's grave!
The thrilling memories of the battle field,
The rattling musketry, and the cannon's sound,
The deadly struggle and the desperate charge,
And the proud form of him who slept
The everlasting slumber in the new made grave,
Dashing through the blinding battle smoke,
The manly voice that urged him in the fight,
The flashing eye and waving sword,
And the noble face that when the day
Was won; these all in the dim twilight
Were bending over him.

This humble, war bruised veteran was the last,
The noblest mourner at the grave that day ;
And the silent prayer he offered
Went up to plead at Heaven's golden gate
For him who was the soldier's friend.
A long way he had come—a long way—
Limping on his crutches through the idle crowd
Which thronged to gaze upon the funeral pageant—
A long way, to breathe his sincere prayer
O'er the noble dead, and shed upon the grave
This touching tribute of a soldier's heart.

· TROUBLE IN HIGH QUARTERS.

During 1865, the writer removed to New York. One evening he met E. S. Sanford, Esq., at the Fifth Avenue Hotel. Mr. Sanford was evidently laboring under some excitement, and reproached me for having asked him to introduce Cavada to Mr. Seward.

I replied: "Sanford, don't get excited; tell me what is the matter."

He said: "I introduced your friend, Cavada, to Mr. Seward at your request. It now turns out that he is a coward, and proofs to that effect have been forwarded to the State Department. You must fix this thing."

I answered: "I *will* fix it. Cavada is no coward. He is not only a brave man, but a gentleman. His error consists, perhaps, in thinking too much of big things, disregarding small ones. I will see that Cavada and you both stand right with the State Department."

The promise thus made was duly performed, as the following will show:

CONSULATE OF THE UNITED STATES OF AMERICA,

TRINIDAD DE CUBA, *April 17th*, 1866.

O. WILSON DAVIS, ESQ.,

New York.

DEAR SIR:

Once more I am called upon to express my thanks to you for important favors, for I am assured that the communications you sent to Washington were strongly conducive to the favorable termination of my difficulties at the Department of State.   They must have been deemed weighty evidence indeed to counteract the misrepresentations of my enemies.

I trust that some day it may be my good fortune to give a more thorough expression to the gratitude for kind offices which places me so deeply in your debt.

I am, sir,

Your very grateful and sincere friend,

FREDERIC F. CAVADA,

U. S. Consul.

He held the position of Consul of the United States at Trinidad de Cuba from the fall of 1864 until February, 1869, when he resigned to take part in the Cuban revolution. This is some evidence that Mr. Seward, who was Secretary of State during this entire period, paid but little attention to the charges that had been lodged in the State Department, though it is evident he examined them.

A GENERAL IN THE CUBAN ARMY.

After Cavada resigned the consulate, he was commissioned as General of the Cuban army for the District of Trinidad, and was subsequently appointed Commander-in-Chief of the Cinco-villas, which included Trinidad, Cienfuegos, Sagua, Villa Clara, Remedios and S'to. Espiritu. When General Jordan returned to the United States, Cavada was appointed Commander-in-Chief of all the Cuban forces, with the title of Chief of the General Staff. His new duties took him from the Cinco-villas Department to Camaguey, where he established his headquarters. His brother, Adolpho, who had been in command of the Cienfuegos District, was appointed to succeed him in the command of the Cinco-villas.

The campaigns of Cavada cover the operations of the past two and a half years in the Cinco-villas Department. It consisted of hard fighting without intermission. The men, though scantily and badly armed and clothed kept the Spaniards at bay, defending their positions in the mountains with wooden cannon, &c., capturing several Spanish garrisons and fortified places, continually harassing the enemy and doing all that the most indomitable energy and heroism could do unsupported and unaided.

At the commencement of the insurrection, he was badly wounded by the accidental discharge of a gun that fell from the hands of one of the sentinels, and for three months endured the most excruciating torment and suffering. During this time, he was concealed in a cave in the mountains with a few of his trusty friends to guard him.

This is not the place, however, to discuss his campaigns in Cuba. They will doubtless be written hereafter by one more competent to do them justice. Any attempt to sketch them with the information that has been received would be a failure.

CAPTURED.

On July 4th, 1871, about eleven o'clock, A. M., the writer was walking up Broadway to keep an appointment, and stopped at a cigar store kept by Victor Giraudy, at 815 Broadway, to buy a cigar. Giraudy is a Cuban, and knew that I had been acquainted with Cavada. He showed -me the following dispatch in the New York Herald of that date :

"*THE WAR IN CUBA.*"

CAPTURE OF GENERAL CAVADA AND ADMIRAL OSORIO BY THE SPANIARDS.

HAVANA, JULY 3rd.

"*The Spanish Gunboat Neptuno captured the insurgent General Fredrico Cavada, while he was trying to leave the Island. He was taken to Puerto Principe for trial. His execution is certain.*"

"*The Neptuno also captured the Cuban Admiral Osorio, who was made famous by capturing the Spanish Coaster Commanditore. Osorio was taken to Neuvitas for trial.*

Three more insurgent leaders on Cayo-Cruz, where Cavada was captured, were surrounded by Spanish seamen and troops and killed."

  * * * * * *

  * * * * * *

Though I had read a morning paper, the foregoing dispatch had escaped my attention. After I read it, Giraudy and the friend who had entered the cigar store with me, expressed the opinion that Cavada had already been shot, because they both knew that he and other Cuban leaders had nearly a year before been tried in their absence by Spanish Court Martial at Havana, and had been sentenced to be shot or garroted whenever captured. At first I was inclined to agree with them in this opinion, but after reading the dispatch carefully, I came to a different conclusion. The dispatch stated that other insurgent leaders captured at the same time *were surrounded by Spanish seamen and troops and killed.* Besides this, it was stated that Cavada *was taken to Puerto Principe for trial.*

Why should this be, except from the fact that Cavada had been " Commander in Chief?" If for this reason, he was not shot *when captured*, as others were, but was sent to Puerto Principe for *trial*, would not a journey to the place of trial and the trial itself occupy several days? These questions I answered satisfactorily to myself in the affirmative, and determined at once to make an effort to save his life. I believed that there was at least a *chance* of his being alive on July the fourth, and determined to make the most of this chance without delay.

Knowing that personally I could do very little, I naturally thought of such men among my acquaintances

as could and would aid me. As it was the Fourth of
July, a national holiday, I knew that such of them as
lived in New York and adjacent cities, would not be
accessible at their places of business either personally or
by telegram, but I resolved to make the most that I
could of the means at hand.

EFFORTS TO SAVE HIS LIFE.

My first thought was to communicate with Cavada's
family in Philadelphia, to let them know I was ready
to co-operate with any movement they might make,
and I telegraphed them. They were, however, absent
from the city, and the special messenger from the
telegraph office, in Philadelphia, was unable to ascertain
their address.

My next thought was of General Sickles, our Minister
at Madrid, with whom I had the good fortune to be
acquainted, and who had known Cavada personally.
About one, P. M., (but about six, P. M., in Spain,) I
sent the following dispatch :

3

NEW YORK, *July 4th*, 1871.

TO GENERAL DANIEL E. SICKLES,
          United States Minister,
                    Madrid, Spain.

Frederic Cavada, Lieutenant-Colonel under you at Gettysburg, now General of Cuban army, has been captured by the Spaniards. Can he be saved?

                    O. WILSON DAVIS,
                              Fifth Avenue Hotel.

———

My next thought was to see some of the Cuban Junta, but I knew none of them personally. Returning to Giraudy's cigar store, I asked him where any of the members of the Junta could be found. He sent his brother with me to Hilario Cisneros, Esq., No. 406 West Twenty-third Street, one of the vice presidents of the Junta, whom I saw. As he spoke English imperfectly, and as I could not speak a word of Spanish, Mr. Giraudy acted as interpreter. Mr. Cisneros manifested great interest in the matter, expressed his belief that Cavada was still alive, and offered on behalf of the Junta to defray any expenses that might be incurred by the movement, which he sincerely hoped might be successful. He did not, however, make any practical suggestions, and after conversing with him, through the interpreter, a few minutes, I took leave.

Soon after leaving Mr. Cisneros, I met a friend who has a large acquaintance with foreigners residing in New York. After he had heard my story, he suggested that I should see General Charles K. Graham, who, he said, had just gone to the Army and Navy Club.

On the mention of his name, I remembered that General Graham was the very man I wanted. He has not only a big heart but a good head, and beside this, he had been Cavada's Brigade Commander and his fellow prisoner at " Libby." I went in search of him and found him just leaving the Club house on his way to dinner, and telling him my errand, he said—" I saw the dispatch in the morning papers, and have spoken to General Franklin, to Major Bundy of the *New York Mail*, and to others, we are to have a special meeting of *the Third Corps Union* to-morrow morning, and will take some action on behalf of Cavada."

I replied,—" General, a town meeting of any kind will not do in this case—to-morrow may be too late."

He said—" I know it, but what else can I do ?"

I replied,—"We *must*, if possible, get General Grant to act without delay. He is a soldier, and if we can lay the case before him properly, I am sure he will do something and that speedily, without regard to the rules of diplomacy or international law. Though I never spoke to him, I know that he did not shoot or permit any one to shoot General Lee or any other rebel officer when they were caught. He will not permit the Spanish authorities in Cuba to shoot Cavada, if it can be prevented. He and Sickles are the only two men in the world who can save Cavada. Sickles has already been appealed to, and we *must* reach General Grant—Come with me to the telegraph office at the Fifth Avenue Hotel, and we will determine on our way there what is to be done."

As we rode to the hotel, Graham said—" General Sheridan is in town, I saw him this morning, and think he his stopping at the Fifth Avenue—let us see him, I know him and think he will help us."

We saw General Sheridan at the hotel. After the case was stated to him, he said without hesitation—" I will do all I can to aid you. I do not wish however, to embarrass the President, but if you see him, tell him that I hope he will do all in his power, officially, to save Cavada's life. I believe that he will do it, but I do not want to ask him to do anything, as I do not know whether any complications could arise from such action. Just state the facts to the President and let him act in his own way. I know him and suggest this as your best course."

From subsequent developments I have reason to believe that General Sheridan telegraphed to General Grant in Cavada's behalf.

We next went to the telegraph office in the hotel and sent the following dispatches :—The operators, Messrs.

J. W. Burnham and C. H. Brown manifested great interest in what we were doing, and did all in their power to get the telegrams "through" without delay.

General Graham had been in correspondence with General Sickles, and knew that he was absent from Madrid. Only the day previous he had received a communication from him. The first dispatch was to London.

NEW YORK, *July 4th,* 1871.

To B. F. STEVENS,
    U. S. Dispatch Agent,
            London.

Where is General Sickles? Very important. Answer.

CHARLES K. GRAHAM,
    Fifth Avenue Hotel.

It was ten P. M., in London, and we did not anticipate a reply until the next day.

NEW YORK, *July 4th,* 1871.

To GEN. HORACE PORTER,
    Long Branch, N. J.

General Cavada, formerly Lieutenant-Colonel of the One Hundred and Fourteenth Pennsylvania Volunteers, lately Commander-in-Chief of the Cuban army, has been captured by the Spanish authorities. He served under my command during the Rebellion and was a good soldier. His brother was likewise on General Humphrey's staff. Can anything be done to save his life?

CHARLES K. GRAHAM,
President Third Corps Union,
Fifth Avenue Hotel.

NEW YORK, *July 4th*, 1871.
To COL. JOHN W. FORNEY,
" Press,"
Philadelphia.

General Cavada, late Lieutenant-Colonel of the One Hundred and Fourteenth Pennsylvania Volunteers has been captured. Telegraph the President and Secretary of State to save his life if possible. Get some leading citizens to unite with you. Lose no time and spare no expense.

CHARLES K. GRAHAM,
O. WILSON DAVIS.

Operator will forward to Col. Forney if he can ascertain where he is.

NEW YORK, *July 4th*, 1871.
To GEN. G. G. MEADE,
Cape May, N. J.

General Cavada, late Lieutenant Colonel of the One Hundred and Fourteenth Pennsylvania Volunteers has been captured. Will you telegraph the President to have his life spared if possible?

CHARLES K. GRAHAM,
Fifth Avenue Hotel.

By the time the foregoing dispatches had been sent, it was 6.30 P. M. and we separated, with the understanding that I would call at General Graham's house before bed time should any answers to the dispatches be received. We also agreed that if the developments of the evening seemed to demand it, we would go to Long Branch during the night, so as to see General Grant early in the morning.

About 7 P. M., I went again to the Fifth Avenue Hotel. On the way, met Mr. Moses Taylor and told him what had transpired. He said he thought everything had been done that it was possible to do. He expressed the most cordial wishes for the success of the measures which had been adopted, and said he would do anything in his power to aid in saving Cavada. If I would only tell him what to do, he was ready to act, and if I thought his influence would be of avail, he offered to sign any telegrams I might write to any person he knew. If I wished to see him later, I was to call at his house before bed time.

During the evening, the city was the scene of the usual Fourth of July excitement. The municipal authorities had provided fireworks at several places, and among others near the Fifth Avenue Hotel, so that I was unable to see any one while the exhibitions were in progress.

Only one reply to our dispatches was received during the evening—the following:

CAPE MAY, *July 4th*, 1871.

CHARLES K. GRAHAM,

    Fifth Avenue Hotel, N. Y.

I have telegraphed the President.

            GEO. G. MEADE.

———

This was received about 10 P. M. About 9 P. M., I had accidentally met James P. Lacombe, Esq., who offered to aid me in the exertions I was making, and said he would go with me to Long Branch that night if necessary.

We went to General Graham's house, and after consultation decided it would be better to postpone any attempt to see the President until the next day.

On July fifth, the following dispatch was sent before 10 A. M.

———

NEW YORK, *July 5th*, 1871.

TO GEN. STEWART VAN VLIET,

    Long Branch, N. J.

Enable O. W. Davis to get an interview with the President about General Cavada, late Commander of the Cuban army, who was captured by a Spanish gun-boat on Sunday. Davis will come to Long Branch to-day and see you.

MOSES TAYLOR.

The following had also been prepared :

New York, July 5th, 1871.

HON. HAMILTON FISH.

Garrison's, N. Y.

General Frederic Cavada, late Commander-in-Chief of the Cuban army, was captured on Sunday by the Spanish authorities while he was trying to escape to this country. He served in the Union Army during the rebellion, and though a native of Cuba, is an American citizen. Will it be possible for the Government to ask the postponement of his execution at least, until he can see his family.

Mr. Taylor said he would sign and send the above with pleasure, but thought that if signed by the Hon. Samuel Sloan, who lived at Garrison's, it would have more effect. Mr. Sloan reached his office about 10.30 A. M., and added to what I had written ;

"I desire this not only for the reasons stated above, but as a personal favor."

SAM. SLOAN.

"Operator please deliver promptly."

The telegram thus amended was forwarded without delay.

About 9 A. M., I had written the following:

New York, July 5th, 1871.

EDWARD S. SANFORD, ESQ.,

Dear Sir:

Frederic F. Cavada, whom you in 1865 had appointed Consul at Cienfuegos, Cuba, has been, as you know, Commander-in-Chief of the Cuban army. The papers yesterday contained a telegram from Havana, saying he had been captured by the Spaniards.

I am trying to get the President to interfere so as to prevent his execution long enough to enable his friends to try to save him. General Sheridan, General Meade and others are helping. Can you not do something? I am going to Long Branch to-day. Have telegraphed General Sickles at Madrid.

Yours truly,

O. WILSON DAVIS,

No. 7 Murray Street.

This was sent to Mr. Sanford by Mr. Lacombe, who reported (about the time Mr. Sloan sent off his dispatch,) that he had seen Mr. Sanford as he was leaving his office to go to Long Branch, who said he would do all he could, and on his arrival at Long Branch would interest John Hoey, Esq., and others. This he did.

After ascertaining that General Grant was not coming to New York that day, and arranging to have all telegrams forwarded, Mr. Lacombe and I went to the foot of Murray Street, and found that the Long Branch boat had gone at 10.30 A. M.,—half an hour earlier than usual, in order to accommodate such persons as wished to attend the races, which were then in progress.

Deeming it important to see General Grant with as little delay as possible, in order that we might be sure our plans had not failed, we took a tug-boat, the "General Rosecranz," and went to Sandy Hook, where a locomotive which was in waiting, took us without delay to the Branch, where we arrived less than one hour and forty minutes from the time we left New York. On reaching the West End Hotel, we found the following telegram :

Madrid July 5th, 1871.

To O. WILSON DAVIS, ESQ.,
New York.

War Minister has telegraphed Captain General to examine Cavada's case and report.

ADEE.

Mr. Adee was in charge of the Legation in the absence of General Sickles.

This was encouraging and was a quicker response to the request made to General Sickles, about eighteen hours previously, than we had anticipated. It yet remained, however, to ascertain what, if any, action had been taken by our government. Fortunately we met Messrs. John Hoey and Edward S. Sanford at the hotel. Mr. Sanford had, as he promised, explained the case to Mr. Hoey, who expressed his willingness to render any assistance in his power. I asked him to go with us to the President's cottage and procure us an interview. This he said he would do with pleasure, but his presence was entirely unnecessary. He had just left the President alone, and knew that he would see me.

We drove at once to General Grant's cottage, and when we asked to see him, were told that he wished to be excused, as he was about to take a drive with his family. I requested the messenger to say that our business was urgent and involved a matter of life and death. General Grant immediately saw us and I said to him, "General, our business relates to General Cavada's case."

He replied, "I have received telegrams from General Meade and other gentlemen on behalf of Cavada, and have already acted in the case."

I felt *instantly* that our success was sure and it was useless to prolong the interview.

I said, "Cavada's friends, sir, thank you for your prompt action. I will detain you no longer."

We returned to the hotel where we soon met General Van Vliet, who was in search of us. After telling him what had been done, he said he would go and ascertain what action General Grant had taken. When he returned to the hotel, he reported that early in the morning, after the receipt of the telegrams about Cavada, the President's Private Secretary had, by his order, telegraphed to the Secretary of State to ask that the execution of any sentence imposed upon Cavada by the Cuban authorities, should be postponed until the circumstances of the case could be inquired into.

This was confirmed by the following dispatch, a copy of which was sent us from New York, during the evening, by General Graham.

LONG BRANCH, *July 5th*, 1871.

To GENERAL CHARLES K. GRAHAM,

Care of O. W. Davis,

New York.

The subject of your telegram has been referred to the Secretary of State.

HORACE PORTER.

We subsequently ascertained that the Secretary of State had telegraphed the request of General Grant to the Spanish Minister at Washington, who, in turn, had telegraphed by cable to the Captain General of Cuba. My efforts thus far having been successful, I felt that Cavada, if alive, would be saved, but being somewhat doubtful of his chances, if tried in Cuba by court martial, I determined to make an effort to have him sent to Madrid for trial, hoping through the agency of Gen. Sickles and others, the King of Spain might be induced to show Cavada some leniency. He was, it is true, a "rebel," in the widest sense of the word, but I remembered that all Christendom had condemned Napoleon for ordering the execution of Andreas Hofer, the Tyrolean Chief, as the meanest act he ever performed as General or Emperor, and though I could call to mind many rebellions, both successful and unsuccessful, since the revolt of the Tyrolese, I could not remember another instance during the present century, at least, of the execution of a rebel Commander-in-Chief. Though I knew that the*rapidity and certainty of Spanish vengeance had been almost proverbial, I hoped that the revolution in Spain, which had resulted in placing the son of the King of Italy upon the throne, would inaugurate in Spain some of the principles of modern civilization and Christian humanity.

Entertaining these views which were, perhaps, intensilied by my interest in Cavada's case, I resolved not to act hastily, but to take the time for reflection which I believed the postponement of the execution of the sentence that had been passed upon him by the authorities of Cuba would afford me. To this end I thought it would be the proper plan to interest as many influential persons as possible in the case, believing that thus it might be possible to induce the American Government to demand that his trial should take place at Madrid, instead of Cuba.

The next morning, July sixth, when returning to New York, I met A. J. Drexel, Esq., of Philadelphia, whom I knew to be a personal friend of the President, and began to put in operation the plan I had determined upon by interesting Mr. Drexel in the case. This was easily done, for he had known Cavada personally, and saying that he approved of my views, promised to do all in his power to carry them out.

The next day, July seventh, the following dispatch was received.

PHILADELPHIA, *July 7th*, 1871.
To GEN. CHARLES K. GRAHAM,
New York.

Five hundred miles from home when your dispatch reached me. Just returned. Will write the President to-day on the subject.

JOHN W. FORNEY.

On the same day Col. Forney wrote to Gen. Graham a letter in which he said, " Please tell Davis and the other friends of Cavada that they will not rely on me in vain."

The next day, July eighth, I received the following dispatch—

LONDON, *July 8th*, 1871.

To O. WILSON DAVIS,
    Attorney at Law,
        No. 7 Murray St., N. Y.

All possible done for Cavada at Madrid by Adee. I have also appealed personally by cable to Serrano for clemency.

SICKLES.

To which I replied :

NEW YORK, *July 8th*, 1871.

To SICKLES,
    London.

Thanks for what you have done. Will it be possible to have Cavada sent to Madrid for trial?

O. WILSON DAVIS.

51

THE EXECUTION.

The morning papers of July eleventh, contained among the "Associated Press" dispatches the following :

CUBA.

EXECUTION OF CAVADA.

HAVANA, *July 10th.*—Cavada was executed on the first inst., at Puerto Principe.

*   *   *   *   *   *

*   *   *   *   *

4

This had a dispiriting effect, but I could not believe it to be true. The dispatch from the same quarter dated Havana, July *third*, stated that Cavada had been captured and sent to Puerto Principe for trial, while this dispatch stated his execution had taken place on the *first*. Between the two, the discrepancy was such that one or the other must have been false. Besides this, I had learned from a reliable source that passengers by steamer from Havana, which left there on the *fifth* of July, stated that a rumor was prevalent in Havana, before they left, that Cavada was to be brought from Puerto Principe to be garroted in Havana. If this were true, then Cavada must have been alive on July *fifth* when the Captain General received dispatches both from Madrid and Washington.

To place the matter beyond doubt, however, efforts were made to telegraph by cable, (in cipher,) both on the *eleventh* and *twelfth* days of July, but they were unsuccessful, because the authorities have control of all the telegraph offices in Cuba, and do not permit any communications "in cipher" even between the operators of the company. Many of Cavada's friends, however, continued to believe that he was alive on July *fifth*, and their belief was sustained by the following publication in the *New York Times* of July *fifteenth*.

"SPECIAL DISPATCH TO THE NEW YORK TIMES."

Washington, July 14*th.*—The report of the execution of the Cuban General Cavada, July *first,* must not be too confidently believed until it receives further confirmation.

It was after that date that Consul General Hall made efforts at Havana from our Government looking towards his release, and Mr. Hall understood that he was alive at that time, if not, the Spanish officers must themselves have either been deceived or deceiving. Advices from Mr. Hall may be expected by mail in a few days.

As the *Times* is known to be an administration journal, many of the friends of Cavada willingly believed that the correspondent's story was authentic, but their hopes were blasted by the following extract from a letter which appeared in the same paper on Friday, July *twenty-first.*

CUBAN AFFAIRS.

FROM OUR OWN CORRESPONDENT.

HAVANA, *Saturday, July* 16*th,* 1871.

*   *   *   *   *   *

DEATH OF CAVADA AND OSORIO.

The following interesting particulars of the capture and execution of the late Gen. Frederico Cavada and Osorio have been related to your correspondent by an

eye-witness, who saw and spoke with both, and wit-
nessed the compliance with the fatal sentence of Spanish
Court-Martial. Osorio had left the interior of the island
some months ago, in company with Bernabe Varona,
alias Bembeta, the young Cuban General who lately
arrived in New York, Osorio being in a most miserable
state of health, and a mass of sores and eruptions from
a kind of scorbut, which is causing such terrible ravages
among the insurgent Cubans, and also from the effects
of an unhealed wound. Osorio refused to state how he
had been left behind by Bembeta, and simply announced
that such had been the fact. He was hid in the woods
and cared for by some Cubans, who could not furnish
him with anything beyond the bare means of subsis-
tence until Gen. Cavada came along and kindly offered
to take him to Nassau or any other secure place, a boat
being then in waiting for the latter gentleman and
another, supposed to have been Mr. Francisco Aguilera,
Ex-Vice-President of the Republic. Everything went
well. They were not seen by any Spanish troops, and
they reached Cayo Cruz in safety, embarking immediately in a two oared boat, and headed for the light-house
on the English key, known as Cayo Lobos, (Wolf Key.)
When in plain sight of the light-house a very stiff breeze
arose, which tossed their boat to and fro, and with the
strong counter-current made the efforts of the rowers
useless, and drove them back toward Cayo Cruz. Cavada

seeing the futility of the attempt to reach Cayo Lobos, then ordered the rowers to return to Cayo Cruz, the boat skimming like a swan over the surface of the water, by the aid of wind and current. At this moment they were sighted by the gun-boat *Vigia,* and shortly after the expeditionists had landed on the key, the Spanish marines were after them. The three other men escaped easily, but *Cavada was too weak to proceed rapidly, and he was, at the same time, sufficiently generous not to leave Osorio to his fate.* The marines sighted them, and an hour after landing they were prisoners in the hands of the Spaniards, who treated them well during their stay on board, the officers giving them provisions and clean clothing. The gun-boat steamed away toward Nuevitas. When the prisoners arrived at Nuevitas, their emaciated appearance and their wretched health excited general pity, and your informant having known both in former years, offered them his services, but as they had been provided with suitable clothing by the commander of the *Vigia,* they declined further aid. Cavada asked for writing materials, and wrote letters to the insurgent Generals, Salomi, Hernandez, Villamli, Penco, Lico, several others, and to his brother, the Cuban General, Adolfo Cavada. Perhaps no man was so much hated by the Spaniards as Cavada, who had earned the soubriquet of the " FIRE KING." Cavada was taken to Puerto Principe on the morning of the thirtieth, and executed on the afternoon of the first. He met his fate like a hero, without bravado or cynicism. Tranquilly he conversed with some friends, and when the fatal hour came he marched, smoking a cigar, erect and proud to the place of execution. When he arrived there he took off his hat, flung it on the ground, and in a loud tone of voice cried, *Adios Cuba, para siempre.* (Good-by Cuba, forever.) A volley was heard, and Frederico Cavada ceased to exist. He persistently refused to see a Catholic priest or to confess, stating that he was not a Catholic either by conviction or practice, *which so incensed the priest that he refused to allow the corpse to be buried in consecrated ground,* and only after a long and bitter quarrel with the Spanish commander, Brig. Gen. Zea, was the matter adjusted. Zea threatened to bury Cavada himself, and send the priest to Havana as a prisoner. The Spanish Post-Captain at Nuevitas, Jacoba Aleman, had in the meantime telegraphed to the Admiral as to what to do with Osorio. The Admiral replied: " He has been sentenced already by a Naval Court as a pirate, and the punishment for pirates is to swing at the yard-arm." But the Spanish Captain had no executioner, so he took it upon himself to have Osorio shot, instead of hung, and the sentence was carried into effect on the morning of the sixth. The shooting party was drawn up. Osorio knelt on the bowsprit of the *Neptuno.* The officer in charge of the party had given instruction that when he raised his sword the men were to get ready, and when he dropped his sword, to fire. He raised his sword, when one of the marines fired, the bullet entering Osorio's head and coming out of the mouth, producing instant death. The others, of course, did not fire, and the body was taken ashore and buried, Osorio having accepted the services of the priest and confessor.

* * * * *

* * * * *

QUASIMODO.